812.54 C529F 2009
John Clancy
Fatboy

Fatboy

by John Clancy

D0746621

Western Wyoming Community College
Hay Library

DISCARDED

A SAMUEL FRENCH ACTING EDITION

SAMUEL FRENCH

FOUNDED 1830

NEW YORK HOLLYWOOD LONDON TORONTO

SAMUELFRENCH.COM

Copyright © 2006, 2009 by John Clancy

ALL RIGHTS RESERVED

CAUTION: Professionals and amateurs are hereby warned that *FATBOY* is subject to a Licensing Fee. It is fully protected under the copyright laws of the United States of America, the British Commonwealth, including Canada, and all other countries of the Copyright Union. All rights, including professional, amateur, motion picture, recitation, lecturing, public reading, radio broadcasting, television and the rights of translation into foreign languages are strictly reserved. In its present form the play is dedicated to the reading public only.

The amateur live stage performance rights to *FATBOY* are controlled exclusively by Samuel French, Inc., and licensing arrangements and performance licenses must be secured well in advance of presentation. PLEASE NOTE that amateur Licensing Fees are set upon application in accordance with your producing circumstances. When applying for a licensing quotation and a performance license please give us the number of performances intended, dates of production, your seating capacity and admission fee. Licensing Fees are payable one week before the opening performance of the play to Samuel French, Inc., at 45 W. 25th Street, New York, NY 10010.

Licensing Fee of the required amount must be paid whether the play is presented for charity or gain and whether or not admission is charged.

Stock licensing fees quoted upon application to Samuel French, Inc.

For all other rights than those stipulated above, apply to Samuel French, Inc., at 45 W. 25th Street, New York, NY 10010.

Particular emphasis is laid on the question of amateur or professional readings, permission and terms for which must be secured in writing from Samuel French, Inc.

Copying from this book in whole or in part is strictly forbidden by law, and the right of performance is not transferable.

Whenever the play is produced the following notice must appear on all programs, printing and advertising for the play: "Produced by special arrangement with Samuel French, Inc."

Due authorship credit must be given on all programs, printing and advertising for the play.

ISBN 978-0-573-69658-9   Printed in U.S.A.   #29068

No one shall commit or authorize any act or omission by which the copyright of, or the right to copyright, this play may be impaired.

No one shall make any changes in this play for the purpose of production.

Publication of this play does not imply availability for performance. Both amateurs and professionals considering a production are strongly advised in their own interests to apply to Samuel French, Inc., for written permission before starting rehearsals, advertising, or booking a theatre.

No part of this book may be reproduced, stored in a retrieval system, or transmitted in any form, by any means, now known or yet to be invented, including mechanical, electronic, photocopying, recording, videotaping, or otherwise, without the prior written permission of the publisher.

IMPORTANT BILLING AND CREDIT
REQUIREMENTS

All producers of *FATBOY must* give credit to the Author of the Play in all programs distributed in connection with performances of the Play, and in all instances in which the title of the Play appears for the purposes of advertising, publicizing or otherwise exploiting the Play and/ or a production. The name of the Author *must* appear on a separate line on which no other name appears, immediately following the title and *must* appear in size of type not less than fifty percent of the size of the title type.

FATBOY received its world premiere at The Assembly Rooms, Edinburgh on August 6, 2004 as part of the Edinburgh Festival Fringe. The set was by Kelly Hanson, costumes by Michael Oberle, lighting by Colin D. Young. Jeff Meyers was the production stage manager, Emily Fishbaine was the assistant director and John Clancy was the director. All music was arranged by Jody Lambert. The cast was as follows:

FATBOY	Mike McShane
FUDGIE	Nancy Walsh
TENANT, PROSECUTOR, SLAVE	Matt Oberg
JUDGE, MINISTER OF FINANCE	David Calvitto
MAILMAN, BAILIFF, INNOCENT, MINISTER OF JUSTICE	Jody Lambert

CHARACTERS

FATBOY - a monster

FUDGIE - his wife

MAILMAN - a mailman

TENANT - a tenant

JUDGE - a judge

BAILIFF - a bailiff

PROSECUTOR - a prosecutor

INNOCENT - an innocent

SLAVE - a slave

MINISTER OF JUSTICE - a minister

MINISTER OF FINANCE - another minister

NOTE ON CASTING: One actor plays **TENANT, PROSECUTOR** and **SLAVE**. Another actor plays **MAILMAN, BAILIFF, INNOCENT** and **MINISTER OF JUSTICE**. Yet another actor plays **JUDGE** and **MINISTER OF FINANCE**.

SET

The play takes place onstage.

NOTES ON SPEED AND VOLUME

Capitalized words are shouted. Not emphasized, SHOUTED. There is a lot of shouting in the play.

The "huge laughter" written into the play must be much louder and go on for much longer than most actors will be comfortable with at first. It is in no way intended to be genuine or "character"-based or anything like that. If committed to, it serves as a Pavlovian cue for the audience and they will find themselves laughing at things they shouldn't. This is, in a way, the point of the whole play.

The play can be extremely harsh on an audience. It should run no longer than seventy minutes or you run the risk of wearing them out and you will lose them in the end.

The actors need to speak quickly; the pauses, unless written in, need to be cut.

GENERAL DESIGN NOTE

Fatboy is not a naturalistic or even realistic work and this must be reflected in the design. In the original Edinburgh and New York productions, a patently false proscenium was built and a red curtain, parting in the middle, was hung. All of the action took place within and in front of the proscenium, except for the entr'actes which took place in front of the closed curtain. The effect was of a live-action, life-sized puppet or Punch and Judy show. The artifice was further highlighted by painted canvas backdrops for each act and two-dimensional, obviously constructed props such as the Judge's gavel and bottle.

The actor playing Fatboy can be any size or shape, as he should be wearing a fatsuit he can remove during the final speech. It is recommended that Fudgie be padded as well, in a way to emphasize her womanly charms and sexuality.

The general look should be as colorful and bright as possible, to give the language and the actors something to work against.

"I intended that, when the curtain went up, the scene in front of the public should be like the mirror in the stories of Madame Leprince de Beaumont in which the wanton saw themselves with horns on the body of a dragon, according to the exaggeration of their vices. It is not surprising that the public should have been astonished at the sight of its ignoble other-self...eternal human imbecility, eternal gluttony, the vileness of instinct elevated into tyranny; the decency, the virtues, the patriotism and the ideals of those who have just dined well."

– Alfred Jarry on *Ubu Roi*, in "Theater Questions" (1897)

(**NOTE:** *Style is broad, vulgar, grand, artificial and quick. Bursts of shouting broken up by melodrama. The lyricism serves to highlight the savagery, the savagery is constant. Every element is overtly theatrical. The lights too bright and rosy, the performers made up mask-like with heavy base, lipstick and eye shadow, the set an obvious construction.*)

ACT ONE – FATBOY THE KING

(The play is set in a poor man's kitchen as imagined by a stage designer. A door unit upstage center, a table, two kitchen chairs, a coat rack, an armchair. Curtain up on **FATBOY** *in armchair, face hidden by newspaper.)*

FATBOY. MOTHERFUCK! Cocksucking fuckheaded motherfucking FUCKS!

FUDGIE. *(shouting from offstage)* Quiet out there!

FATBOY. I HAVE BEEN INSULTED!

FUDGIE. SHUT IT YOU FAT BASTARD!

FATBOY. *(lowers paper, stares out at audience, brooding)* A quiet morning shattered. A newborn day aborted at the moment of birth. PANCAKES!

FUDGIE. *(offstage)* SHUT IT!

FATBOY. *(resumes brooding)* A conspiracy, clearly. An obvious and clumsy attempt to unsettle. My enemies, a cabal of cocksucking whores, lash out at me even here. SAUSAGE!

FUDGIE. *(entering)* There is no sausage, you fat wretched bastard.

FATBOY. BACON!

FUDGIE. YOU'VE EATEN IT ALL YOU MONSTER YOU DUNGHEAP YOU MAN.

FATBOY. Slander. Slander and lies and more. Have you read the paper today?

FUDGIE. Other people's business bores me. I have business of my own.

FATBOY. I have sounded out each sentence, squinted out each semicolon and NOTHING. No word. No scrap. Not the smallest mention of me.

FUDGIE. Why that speaks volumes, dear. You are nothing. You barely exist.

FATBOY. I AM FATBOY AND I AM KING.

FUDGIE. I often forget about you myself. But then, of course, your stench reminds me that yes, sadly, you continue to live, leech-like and horrid, a barnacle on my ship of state.

FATBOY. LEECHES! FRIED LEECHES IN BEER BATTER AND NOW YOU WRECK YOU SHREW!

FUDGIE. THERE IS NO MONEY FOR FOOD! OR CLOTH-ING OR SHELTER OR HEAT! We spent our last dime last night throwing it at the clowns.

FATBOY. Scattered them good, though.

FUDGIE. O yes, they scampered.

FATBOY. Filthy white-faced fucks.

FUDGIE. Outcasts and freaks of the world.

FATBOY. A clown is an abomination.

FUDGIE. A warning to the rest not to stray.

FATBOY. Sit here on my lap, dear, and let's pretend we're young.

FUDGIE. Haul your fat ass up, dear, and go and bring back coin.

FATBOY. Dance for me, my pumpkin.

FUDGIE. Make some money, pig.

FATBOY. Is that all you can talk about? Money money money money? Is that all there is to this life? What of art? Beauty? Truth?

(A pause as she considers the question and then they laugh hugely at the joke, slapping their knees and wiping tears from their eyes.)

FUDGIE. *(recovering)* Ah, you fat fucker, you can still make me laugh.

FATBOY. Wait. Justice! Honor! Love!

FUDGIE. No. Better the first way.

FATBOY. MUST YOU ALWAYS CRITICIZE?

FUDGIE. FAT UGLY STUPID MAN!

FATBOY. Every day. Every day the same. No peace. No quiet contemplation. No chance for a moment to gather slowly and present itself to me. Always cursing. Always raised voices and clenched fists and this caterwauling wretch of a wife stomping about and this second-rate wreck of a life spooling away and always the same, day after day after day after day after-wait, what's the date today?

FUDGIE. The first.

FATBOY. Of the month?

FUDGIE. Yes.

FATBOY. It's check day.

FUDGIE. No.

FATBOY. It is. The check comes on the first of the month.

FUDGIE. That's today!

FATBOY. I know!

FUDGIE. We're saved!

FATBOY. HA! And you were suggesting I work.

FUDGIE. The check. My god. I had forgotten.

FATBOY. You must have faith in this world and its ways. You must never, never despair.

FUDGIE. We can eat. Turn the phone back on. Buy things from the television.

FATBOY. I myself am a fortress of faith. I believe. I believe in all things.

FUDGIE. We'll re-decorate. Throw out all this trash and wreckage and create a paradise.

FATBOY. All sects, all dogmas, all opinions and gossip. All is true, if you believe.

FUDGIE. *(sweetly)* About the check, dear Fatboy?

FATBOY. What of it, harpy?

FUDGIE. What is it for, again?

FATBOY. Royalties.

FUDGIE. But your blood is common.

FATBOY. Now, yes, but once it was rare and it boiled from my veins out onto the page and I spattered masterworks all day.

FUDGIE. You're a writer, then?

FATBOY. DON'T INSULT ME! I was young and knew no better.

FUDGIE. When I was young I was wise.

FATBOY. You were never young, you horrible cow.

FUDGIE. I HAVE PHOTOGRAPHS!

FATBOY. FORGERIES!

FUDGIE. FAT BASTARD!

(They rush at each other in mortal combat, grapple and then are interrupted by a call from the door.)

MAILMAN. *(offstage)* Special delivery!

FATBOY. Hush.

FUDGIE. My god.

MAILMAN. *(offstage)* Special delivery for Fatboy! Royalty check for Fatboy!

FATBOY. The check.

FUDGIE. Sweet holy crippled Christ.

(FATBOY disengages from FUDGIE, opens door. MAILMAN with envelope.)

FATBOY. *(deeply suspicious)* Yes?

MAILMAN. Fatboy?

FATBOY. Perhaps.

FUDGIE. It's him, it's him.

(FATBOY spins and glares at FUDGIE, she drops her gaze.)

MAILMAN. I have a special delivery for Fatboy.

FATBOY. Who sent you?

MAILMAN. The dispatcher.

FATBOY. Hand it over and no one gets hurt.

MAILMAN. Are you Fatboy, then?

FATBOY. None of your impertinence, dickhead. Give me what is mine.

(**MAILMAN** *hands over envelope, holds out clipboard.*)

MAILMAN. Sign here.

(**FATBOY** *makes X on clipboard.*)

MAILMAN. First and last.

(**FATBOY** *makes second X on clipboard.*)

MAILMAN. God bless you and keep you both.

FATBOY. *(slamming door in his face)* I WILL NOT HAVE THAT TALK IN MY HOUSE!

FUDGIE. It's true. The check. Sweet merciful jug-headed Jesus.

FATBOY. *(holding envelope high)* SALVATION!

FUDGIE. *(trying to get check)* SCENTED SOAP SHAPED LIKE FLOWERS!

FATBOY. ALCOHOL! CIGARETTES! BACON! MINE! MINE! MINE!

(**FATBOY** *devours envelope.*)

FATBOY. Ah. Consumption.

FUDGIE. You fat idiot. You ate the check.

FATBOY. I feel a nap coming on. *(He collapses to floor, snoring loudly and theatrically.)*

FUDGIE. *(kicks him)* Is this it then, always? Forever fighting with the fat bastard over scraps of money not mine? Grinding away the time like two teeth clenched, gnashing away in the dark? Where are my children to comfort and console me in this my hour of need?

FATBOY. You ate your firstborn and drove the rest away.

FUDGIE. You're sleeping! No talking while sleeping!

FATBOY. I'm talking in my sleep!

FUDGIE. You are not! You are silent in your sleep you fat bastard!

FATBOY. WHORE!

FUDGIE. MUTE BASTARD! Yes it is true I ate my first one but such a sweet little morsel he was. All pink and plump and perfect. The others I don't remember, ungrateful and demanding, I'm sure, and clumsy and needy like all children are. Rolling around on the floor in their filth and not able to support their own heads. How in Christ could they ever support me?

FATBOY. *(rising)* Most refreshing lying there pretending to sleep. Much more refreshing than actual sleep, the paralysis and dreams and despair.

FUDGIE. Do you dream, horror?

FATBOY. Of heaven.

FUDGIE. Is it nice?

FATBOY. If you like that sort of thing.

FUDGIE. I dream of death.

FATBOY. Yours or someone who matters?

FUDGIE. I'm always alone in my dreams.

FATBOY. Heaven, death, bedtime stories. What are we having for lunch?

FUDGIE. Nothing if you don't make some money. You fat disgusting monster.

FATBOY. What am I, a mint? Some kind of mint? Do you have any mints?

FUDGIE. Earn some money, monster.

FATBOY. Gum? A candy wrapper? Something goddamn it?

FUDGIE. We are destitute, you lumbering wreck. We have nothing but the clothes on our back and the furniture here before you.

FATBOY. Am I to eat a chair? Am I to devour a table, you harpy, you witch?

FUDGIE. GO. AND GET. MONEY.

(She exits.)

FATBOY. Women. Always so cryptic. I'M NOT A MIND-READER, YOU KNOW! She wants something from me, of course, that much is obvious, they all do. Greedy greedy give me give me. *(He begins to absentmindedly gnaw the chair.)* But never a thought for poor Fatboy. Never, what would you like, sweet Fatboy? Always this way, all my life, all my lives, every tick of time. As a boy, left to riot, as a man left to rot. Cocksuckers. Asshole fuckheaded cocksuckers. Always the burden. Always the load. I'M EATING A CHAIR! HAS IT COME TO THIS? *(continues snacking on chair)* Well I say no more. I say fuck all y'all and fuck you twice from behind. I am not a beast of burden. I am not a servant or a Slave. I am Fatboy and I AM GOD. I will take what I need, I will take what I deserve, I will take whatever I see. I shall be rich, I shall be respected and I shall be fed. *(He tosses chair down, strides to the coat rack, puts on coat.)* WHERE IS MY HAT?

FUDGIE. *(offstage)* YOU ATE IT!

FATBOY. NOT THAT ONE! MY "NOW I SHALL BE RESPECTED" HAT!

FUDGIE. *(enters)* You're going to be respected?

FATBOY. Not without that hat.

FUDGIE. Who would respect you?

FATBOY. Various and sundry. All God's creatures.

FUDGIE. *(dismissively)* *Them.* Get some money while you're out there. Or shoot the President.

FATBOY. My hat, harpy?

FUDGIE. Shoved up your fat ass, I believe.

FATBOY. *(searches with both hands behind him, pulls out top hat)* Ah. *(puts it on)* Warm. How do I look?

FUDGIE. The spitting image of yourself.

FATBOY. Don't insult me. And don't sleep with anyone while I'm gone.

FUDGIE. Shall I wait until you're back then?

FATBOY. I SHALL BE RESPECTED! *(walks grandly into door, falls down)* MOTHERFUCK! *(gets to his feet)* I'm off, then.

FUDGIE. Ta-ta.

FATBOY. *(exiting)* VICTORY! HONOR! PANCAKES!

FUDGIE *(swooning)* I love that ugly sack of shit and yet I think of murder. Just stab him in the head forty or fifty times and watch him drop away dead. Beat him with a baseball bat until my arm gets tired. Suffocate him in his fitful sleep. I have myself to think of, after all. I was not born, brought screaming into this world, delivered like a package, to be poor. My parents' indiscretion was not to result in this. I am of noble lineage. I have the charts. My profile belongs on coins. I'm the brains of this outfit is what I'm saying and don't you ever forget it. He can strut, he can swagger, but I'm deep below. I'm tracking it out ten moves away. Proof? I'll give you proof. *(She grabs newspaper.)* Here, in the classifieds, what is this among the desperate and depraved? "Room to let. Wrong side of town. Professionals only, please." I always could turn a phrase, that last part is poetry. I placed the ad, got him out of the house and now sit back like a queen. *(She sits regally. A knock on the door.)* My god it worked. Ten words printed in the morning paper and a professional knocks on my door. This is truly the time of modern marvels, the apex of civilization. *(a knock on the door)*

(to audience) Don't tell him about Fatboy. I live alone in dignified squalor. I'm a woman to be pitied and paid. Sit up straight and look presentable. I'll do the talking.

(Opens door, TENANT stands there, Gilbert and Sullivan tenor type, maybe tight pants, ruffled shirt, blond coiffed wig. Underneath, shabby, dirty, untrustworthy type.)

FUDGIE. *(feigning innocence and distraction)* Yes hello, hello yes?

TENANT. I saw the ad in the paper.

FUDGIE. Ad? Ad in the paper?

TENANT. Yes. "Room to let. Wrong side of town. Et cetera."

FUDGIE. Et cetera? O yes. Of course. Et cetera. "Professionals Only Please."

TENANT. Exactly. Yes. May I come in?

FUDGIE. Are you, then?

TENANT. Am I?

FUDGIE. Professional?

TENANT. I am.

FUDGIE. Come in, young man, come in.

(**TENANT** *enters.*)

TENANT. My dear woman, this room is a shambles.

FUDGIE. My dear man, this is not the room.

TENANT. Ah. Then forgive my judgment.

FUDGIE. Are you a judge, then?

TENANT. A judge? O no.

FUDGIE. A lawyer, a court reporter, a bailiff?

TENANT. I avoid the law whenever possible, ma'am.

FUDGIE. A prudent course of action. Are you a doctor, an accountant, a dean of some school?

TENANT. I am none of those things, ma'am. I resent the implications.

FUDGIE. I will not have a merchant under my roof.

TENANT. So the roof comes with it, too?

FUDGIE. Four walls, a roof, one floor.

TENANT. A door?

FUDGIE. For those deserving. Are you a banker, an ombudsman, a seller of stocks and bonds?

TENANT. I have been many things, ma'am, but none that you have mentioned.

FUDGIE. Please bore us then with your life and times.

TENANT. My life is a trial I must endure. My times are dark and troubled.

FUDGIE. *(to audience)* This stranger moves me somehow. Is it his wig or something deeper? My every thrust he parries. I'll suss him this time sure. *(to* **TENANT***)* State your occupation and none of your poetry now.

TENANT. I kill people for money.

FUDGIE. A lot of money or not so much?

TENANT. A tremendous amount. I do it right. I am a professional.

FUDGIE. Well that's the word I'm looking for, for the sake of St. Malcolm the Mick. Welcome, young man. Three months upfront and a security deposit of one.

TENANT. Four months then total?

FUDGIE. *(to audience)* A mathematician, too. My heart beats polyrhythmic.

TENANT. Will you take a check?

(A pause as she considers the question and then they laugh hugely at the joke.)

FUDGIE. And a funnyman as well. Cash, now, and don't start taking off your shirt and flexing that lovely flesh.

TENANT. *(handing her a sack of money and taking off his shirt)* Warm in here.

FUDGIE. The heat is not included.

TENANT. What is included, temptress?

FUDGIE. As I said, four walls, one floor, the ceiling and… *(She trails off coquettishly.)*

TENANT. A door?

FUDGIE. O sir.

TENANT. A door to close and dance behind?

FUDGIE. We have no cabaret license.

TENANT. A door to lock so those outside can't witness what happens within?

FUDGIE. Don't take off your pants, now, I implore you, let me help.

(TENANT kicks off shoes as she unsnaps his pants and pulls them down.)

TENANT. Did I tell you I kill for a living?

FUDGIE. Get them off get them off get them off.

TENANT. Barehanded mostly. No weapon to clean or conceal.

FUDGIE. Come with me now my killer.

TENANT. A hand around the neck. A squeeze. A twist.

FUDGIE. Come with me to your room.

TENANT. Am I in, then?

FUDGIE. Ah, soon. Soon my murdering boy. I'll do you like a dirty deed I've dreamed of all my days

TENANT. And I'll do you like a duty I would rather leave undone.

(**FUDGIE** *drags* **TENANT** *off stage right.* **FATBOY** *bangs the front door open, bloody, wads of cash in his hands.*)

FATBOY. MOTHERFUCK! COCKSUCKING FUCKHEADED PIECE OF SHIT FUCKS! I go into the world harmless, wishing none ill will or folly and am repaid for my kindness with blood. Not mine, thank god, but still.

FUDGIE. *(offstage amidst much scraping and banging)* O MY GOD, YES!

TENANT. *(offstage)* WAIT!

FATBOY. *(He glances offstage and then continues.)* I walk to the center of town, declare myself king, ask for what is due me and am given…what? Riches? Kisses? Titles and deeds and keys to the vaults hidden deep? No, none of these, no. I am given scorn.

FUDGIE. *(offstage)* GIVE IT TO ME, YES!

TENANT. I WILL, I WILL, JUST WAIT!

FATBOY. I am given laughter. Cold, cruel, "HAHS" and then I am left alone. In a crowd of my subjects, a hive of those below me, alone, avoided, shunned.

FUDGIE. *(offstage)* BABBLING BLUE-EYED JESUS!

TENANT. *(offstage)* HOLD STILL, WOMAN!

FUDGIE. *(offstage)* SWEET SPASTIC MOTHER OF CHRIST!

TENANT. *(offstage)* FOR GOD'S SAKE HUSH!

FATBOY. And so I walk to the courthouse. Immense, gray-stoned, forbidding. I climb the marble stairs, push open the massive door and stand in the echoing lobby. And amplified by the architect's art I whisper I Am Fatboy. Bow Before Me Or Die. My reasoned offer ripples off the walls and reaches every ear. They turn, as one, as many, as all, and look upon their ruler.

FUDGIE. *(offstage)* GREAT GURGLING GOOGLE-EYED GOD!

TENANT. *(offstage)* I'LL KILL YOU, YOU KNOW! I WILL!

FATBOY. QUIET IN THERE OR I'LL CRUSH YOU! *(scraping and banging stops offstage)* All eyes on me now. All palms itching. All spines stiff. An eternity passes, silent and still, and then one steps out from the throng. He is old, palsied, hunched by the weight of his years, but his eyes are clear and his voice is strong as he shouts, "Get out of here you madman or we shall call the authorities."

*(**FUDGIE** peeks out from stage left.)*

My laughter explodes like a hydrogen isotope and I see him physically shrink half a foot as I bellow out "Authorities? I am the Authority. I AM FATBOY AND I AM DEATH.

*(**TENANT** peeks out next to **FUDGIE**.)*

I AM THE DESTROYER OF WORLDS. And with this I stride forward and begin the work of the day.

*(During the following speech, **TENANT** and **FUDGIE** cross slowly towards **FATBOY**, captivated by the tale. **TENANT**'s shirt is on inside out, he has no pants, **FUDGIE**'s skirt is down around her ankles.)*

The old man stands fast and I admire his courage in the second before I snap his chicken neck. His murder unfreezes the crowd and half run shrieking away and half rush towards me, hands out, mouths moving, but there seems to me no sound. Slow motion, silent enemies drifting into my grasp. I deliver death like a dutiful postman, each man getting his own. They tear and claw at me and there are arms around my legs and faces pressed against mine but I am Fatboy. I prevail. It is still again and sound comes back, the ragged breath of the dying, the weeping of those still alive, hiding in the shadows and the corners of the room. From one shadow a young girl steps, pretty in her young girl's dress, her young girl's hair held back from her face by a bow. She crosses to a crumpled corpse, kneels and then looks to me. "My daddy", she says. "Is dead," I say, "and you will be too, some day. Now help me get the money from their coats or that some day is now." Working together, we clear the lot, her small hands much

quicker than mine and soon she's enjoying the game. The
search, the discovery, the growing pile of green. When we
are done, I slip her a hundred and she curtsies and asks for
more. So I make a fist and raise it high and smash it down
on her head. She falls like a puppet whose strings I've cut.
I take the bill from her lifeless hand and walk through
the pooling blood to the door. It is a beautiful day, if you
like that sort of thing, sunshine and blue sky and a gentle
breeze from the West. I walk home the long way, through
the old section, stopping to murder and thieve. Most smile
and nod when they see me, relieved, I think, that I am
finally here, that they are finally done. Some run. These I
chase and the fastest get away. All in all, bloody work. Now
make me some pancakes. Who's this?

TENANT. *(offering his hand)* A fellow bare-hands man. Well-done.

FATBOY. *(not taking his hand)* What are you doing in my
home? What is he doing in my home?

FUDGIE. More than you've done in years, fat bastard. Let
me have the cash.

FATBOY. *(handing her the wads of bloody notes which she begins
to count)* You look like a strapping fellow.

TENANT. I've strapped a few in my time.

FATBOY. And why do you stand before me? Why are my
eyes assaulted by the sight of your self?

TENANT. I am your new tenant, sir.

FATBOY. Are you mad? Is he mad?

FUDGIE. He's lovely, you monstrous beast, and he knows
how to use it, too.

FATBOY. My new tenant? I haven't an old and yet you're the new?

TENANT. I answered your ad in the paper.

FATBOY. My ad in the paper? Did I run an ad saying "Strapping young fools only, pants not required"? WHAT IS
THE MEANING OF THIS?

FUDGIE. I'm renting out your study so that we can eat and
frolic and this fine young killer answered the ad. Of
course, now what with this fortune, we don't need the
income, but my god he's hung like a donkey so I think
we'll keep him, dear.

FATBOY. My study is sacred.

FUDGIE. You never use it, pig.

FATBOY. Where will I keep my books? My years of research and notes?

FUDGIE. I threw them out yesterday while you were choking on something.

FATBOY. GODDAMNED OLIVES! THEY SHOULD SAY IF THEY HAVE PITS!

FUDGIE. *(finishing the count and beginning to become thoughtful)* This is a lot of money, but I have a feeling that there's more.

TENANT. There's a world of it out there, if you know how to ask.

FATBOY. So you'll be living here, then?

TENANT. I'm paid up for three months.

FATBOY. And sleeping with this horrible woman?

TENANT. I don't know what you mean, sir.

FATBOY. YOU'RE NOT WEARING PANTS AND HER SKIRT'S BELOW HER KNEES. I AM NOT BLIND. A little near-sighted, I think. Which is it when you can't see far away, but up close is fine?

TENANT. That's near-sighted. You can see what's near.

FATBOY. Makes sense. PAY ME FOR WHAT YOU HAVE TAKEN.

FUDGIE. *(still figuring out loud)* This is plenty of money, but still…

TENANT. Taken? I took nothing.

FUDGIE. Still, if there's more, why then…

FATBOY. Be reasonable, young man. Out in the street, in an alley or a park, it would run you twenty dollars, fifty if she's fine. But you had a room. Four walls, a ceiling and a floor. You had privacy and leverage. Now, granted, she's a sea lion and a horror and a cow, an affront to all that's holy and good, but still. I have to ask for thirty.

TENANT. You should pay me, sir. It was an act of charity and courage.

FUDGIE. It should all be mine, really. Others shouldn't have things. Others should make things and give things. To me. What on earth would others do with things?

FATBOY. Thirty dollars or hell's unleashed.

TENANT. Damn you, sir. Not a penny.

FATBOY. Three thousand pennies or your life.

TENANT. I should warn you, sir, I am a professional.

FATBOY. And I should warn you, fuckface, I'm an enthusiast.

FUDGIE. Others should serve and be grateful.

FATBOY. STRAPPING TENANT FUCK!

TENANT. FAT CUCKOLD BASTARD!

(They fight, horribly, realistically, loudly as **FUDGIE** *rises and with money in hands speaks her reverie.)*

FUDGIE. Others should willingly, instinctively, give all they have to the fat man and me or they should be unmade. We want things, after all. We have desires. We're only human and we desire it all. There are things not yet made and those we desire as well, those most of all, I believe, and we shall have them, yes. We shall have everything and all shall serve or we'll crush them like insects, like beetles 'neath our boots. And if there are things we don't desire, things that don't please us or are shoddy or confuse us, then those things shall be crushed as well. Nothing should be that we don't desire, nothing should exist that we can't own and enjoy. A bonfire of all the things we don't want will lick the night sky and make bright the dark heavens above. And below that dark heaven we'll reign. Fatboy the King and his bride, Queen Fudgie the First.

TENANT. *(his hands around* **FATBOY**'s *hands wrapped around his neck)* All right, sir, you've won.

FUDGIE. Haven't you killed him yet?

FATBOY. One sec. *(snaps* **TENANT**'s *neck)* There it is. *(***TENANT** *collapses to floor, dead.)* What's for dinner? I'm starving.

FUDGIE. Tonight we dine, fat bastard.

FATBOY. My dear, you look radiant with all that money. Give it back now.

FUDGIE. *(admiringly)* And you with the blood of strangers and slaves, smeared on you like jelly on toast.

FATBOY. JELLY! TOAST! CHEESECAKE AND PIE!

FUDGIE. You must kill more, my monster.

FATBOY. You're not the boss of me.

FUDGIE. The world awaits your slaughter.

FATBOY. Let it wait. I'm hungry. FOOD GODDAMNIT AND NOW!

FUDGIE. Did you shoot the President?

FATBOY. Seemed like such a waste.

FUDGIE. A waste, you horror, why?

FATBOY. They'll just elect another.

FUDGIE. Who will, pig?

FATBOY. Anyone. The rabble. Citizens.

FUDGIE. *(dismissively) Them.*

FATBOY. Give me the money, whore.

FUDGIE. It's mine now, pig. Get your own.

FATBOY. Surely there's enough if we share.

(A pause as she considers and then they laugh hugely at the joke.)

FUDGIE. *(wiping tears of laughter from her eyes)* Ah, you fat fucker, you do make me laugh.

FATBOY. *(embracing her while reaching for the cash)* And you make me choke with revulsion.

FUDGIE. *(trying to wriggle away)* You're getting blood on my blouse.

FATBOY. Give me the money, woman.

FUDGIE. *(struggling)* GET YOUR OWN! IT'S MINE!

FATBOY. I WILL NOT BE DENIED!

FUDGIE. FAT BASTARD!

FATBOY. WHORE!

(They struggle, he grabs the money and begins to devour it.)

FATBOY. MMMM! TASTY TASTY!

FUDGIE. STOP IT FAT BASTARD! NO!

FATBOY. MORE! MORE! MORE!

(His laughter and her protests rise as the curtain drops.)

FIRST ENTR'ACTE

(FATBOY and FUDGIE step in front of curtain, waving and bowing to the crowd.)

FATBOY. We'd just like to take this opportunity to thank the author, Tom Clancy, for putting our lives on stage.

FUDGIE. We loved his *Hunt for Red October* and are naturally impressed with his encyclopedic knowledge of technological warfare.

FATBOY. We realize that this is a departure for him and we're honored that –

(A note is thrust through the curtain. FATBOY takes it.)

What's this? John Clancy. It's John Clancy. Not Tom.

FUDGIE. John Clancy the cook?

FATBOY. The nationally recognized chef and pastry-maker?

FUDGIE. It must be.

FATBOY. His recipes are prose masterpieces.

FUDGIE. His lists of ingredients haikus.

FATBOY. HE MAKES CAKES! AND COOKIES AND CRUSTS AND PIES!

FUDGIE. Something very sexy about a man who cooks. You want to lift up his apron and feast.

FATBOY. In any event, it is an honor to be portrayed.

FUDGIE. Although we must caution you that this is fiction.

FATBOY. A fictionalization.

FUDGIE. Lies.

FATBOY. Slander and character assassination.

FUDGIE. We shall sue and certainly win.

FATBOY. In actual life I am slender.

FUDGIE. And I a blushing virgin.

FATBOY. Well, no, you're a whore, he's got that right.

FUDGIE. You're a fat tub of shit.

FATBOY. Your hips are permanently splayed, you wanton wretched witch.

FUDGIE. Fat fat fucker.

FATBOY. HARPY!

FUDGIE. MONSTER!

FATBOY. WOMAN!

FUDGIE. MAN!

(Enormous hooks come from either end of stage and drag them off, screaming.)

ACT TWO – FATBOY IN CHAINS

(Curtain up on the courtroom, **JUDGE** *center stage up high,* **PROSECUTOR** *at table stage left.)*

JUDGE. *(banging gavel)* Order! Order in the Court! This most august session of the War Crimes Tribunal is hereby called to order. Can I get anyone a drink?

PROSECUTOR. No thank you, your honor.

JUDGE. Little something?

PROSECUTOR. No, sir, I'm fine.

JUDGE. Take the edge off?

PROSECUTOR. No, really, I'm good.

JUDGE. All right. Bring in the accused.

*(**FATBOY** enters in chains, dragged on by **BAILIFF**.)*

FATBOY. MOTHERFUCK! PIECE OF SHIT ASSFUCKING FUCKS! Release me now and your deaths, though horrific, will not be televised.

PROSECUTOR. You're in no position to make deals, sir!

JUDGE. Can I get you a drink?

FATBOY. *(to **PROSECUTOR**)* Do you know whom you are addressing, dickhead?

PROSECUTOR. A foul and murderous beast.

JUDGE. Little taste?

FATBOY. A free man stands before you, slave.

PROSECUTOR. A free man draped in chains.

FATBOY. I am History Incarnate. You are not even a footnote.

PROSECUTOR. A history written in blood is a signed confession in time.

FATBOY. INSIGNIFICANT FUCK!

PROSECUTOR. MONSTER!

(They rush at each other, **FATBOY** *restrained by* **BAILIFF**.)*

JUDGE. *(pounding gavel)* ORDER! ORDER IN THIS COURT! *(to* **BAILIFF***)* How about you, something?

BAILIFF. No, your honor.

JUDGE. Well, shit. This is going to be a long day. *(takes out flask, drinks)* Allrighty then. The prosecution will read the charges.

FATBOY. I object, you asshole fuckhead.

JUDGE. On what grounds?

FATBOY. I object, first of all, to these chains. If you are to chain me, I insist on actual chains, not these cheap theatrics. What is this, I ask you, a non-union tour of A Christmas Carol? "Scrooge, Scrooo-ooooge." This is horseshit and I will not abide it. Secondly, if you are to sit up there for the entire act, I will be completely upstaged and I am the title character. I AM FATBOY AND I AM TITULAR. I respect the stagecraft and understand that the scene must be staged this way, but I must insist upon better lighting. Spotlight, pink gel, to follow me wherever I roam. *(A spotlight clicks on.)* And thirdly, I object on general principle, I object because this is objectionable, I object because it is my objective to do so, I object because you are assholes and fuckheads and I am your rightful God. Fuck all y'all and fuck your grandmas twice. Thank you.

JUDGE. Well said, sir. However, I wasn't really paying attention, so I'm going to have to overrule your objection. Can I get you a drink?

FATBOY. FREEDOM, FUCKHEAD!

JUDGE. You're a shouting person, aren't you? Shouty shouty shouty. I like that in a defendant. Gives the illusion of drama.

PROSECUTOR. Your honor?

JUDGE. Yes?

PROSECUTOR. May I read the charges?

JUDGE. You're sort of a stickler, aren't you? Shouty and Stickly. I wonder who will win.

PROSECUTOR. The charges, sir?

JUDGE. By all means, Stickly. The charges indeed.

(During the following speech the **JUDGE** *pours himself a drink, downs it.* **FATBOY** *takes out a cigarette, searches for matches and finding none, shrugs and eats the cigarette. No one pays the slightest attention to the charges.)*

PROSECUTOR. The accused, Fatboy the Monster, variously known as Fat Man, Fatty Fatty, The Fat Bastard, Fathead, Farthead (sic), That Man There, Horror Beyond Words, Boogala-Boogala-Boogala (sic), He Whose Face is Death, Stinky Pete, Whoa There Nellie and The Drifter, is accused of the following crimes, felonies, malfeasances and acts of outrage: To wit: rape, murder, looting, genocide, gross accounting irregularities, predatory lending, fraud, intention to commit fraud, illegal wiretapping, extortion, intention to commit extortion, loan-sharking, racketeering, armed robbery of citizens and state banks and post offices, the theft of sacred objects, receiving stolen goods, selling stolen goods, overt intention to commit global gangsterism, willing and knowing permission and encouragement of slave labor, intentional and institutional boorishness and profound criminal stupidity. How do you plead?

FATBOY. May I address the court?

JUDGE. You may.

FATBOY. Thank you, you enormous asshole. May I just say that I AM FATBOY AND I AM THE LAW. You are all assholes. Assholes of the world, I address you as your king, as your god, as your destiny and destroyer. I see here before me assholes from every hellhole on earth. I welcome you, I call you assholes, I spit on your traditions and faiths. You are assholes, your parents are assholes, your heroes, statesmen and ancestors are complete and perfect assholes. Assholes, what I ask for here today is very simple. From this day forward, you all must agree to shut the fuck up, fuck yourselves, and stay the fuck out of my way. I AM FATBOY. In short, fuck all y'all, you big, big assholes. Thank you.

PROSECUTOR. So you plead guilty to these crimes?

FATBOY. What you call crimes, I call freedom. I ask you, asshole, is it a crime to breathe the harsh air of liberty? Is it a crime to recognize injustice and act to right what is wrong? Is it a crime to grab an old woman by the shoulders, lift her up into the air, shake her a few times and then throw her to the ground, snapping her bones like kindling for a fire? Then leap into the air and come down with both boots squarely on the old woman and stomp around there for awhile? Then go through her pockets and find what small fortune she hid? If these things are crimes, then I plead guilty. Guilty by reason of divine right. Guilty by reason of magnitude. Guilty by the simple fact of being too large for your puny laws to apply. Guilty guilty guilty.

JUDGE. I must warn you, sir, that these charges are most severe. There are certain rights, inalienable rights, human rights that must be upheld. Every life, no matter how small, is precious and must be protected.

(A pause as the courtroom considers and then all burst into huge laughter.)

FATBOY. Good one, fuckhead.

JUDGE. Yeah, I love that bit. So now. You realize by pleading guilty you face the death penalty?

FATBOY. I did not realize that, asshole. May I change my plea?

JUDGE. Certainly.

FATBOY. Innocent as a schoolgirl soaping herself in the sink.

JUDGE. The plea is so entered. Does anyone need a drink? No? Does anyone have any playing cards? No. Jesus. The prosecution may call its first witness.

PROSECUTOR. The prosecution calls the defendant's wife and accomplice, Queen Fudgie the First.

*(**FUDGIE** enters, dressed to the nines, smiling, waving, blowing kisses to the crowd.)*

FUDGIE. Thank you, thank you, thank you all.

BAILIFF. Do you swear to tell the truth, the whole truth and nothing but the truth?

FUDGIE. A lady never swears.

BAILIFF. Fair enough.

FATBOY. I object. That's no lady, that's my wife.

(huge laughter bit)

FUDGIE. Ah, you fat fucker, you can still make me laugh.

FATBOY. Wait, better, I object, that's no lady, that's a horrible fucking beast.

FUDGIE. No, better the first way.

FATBOY. MUST YOU ALWAYS CRITICIZE?

FUDGIE. FAT UGLY STUPID GUILTY WAR CRIMINAL!

FATBOY. WHORE!

JUDGE. SILENCE! Can I get you a drink?

PROSECUTOR. State your name and your relationship to the accused.

FUDGIE. I'll take the fifth.

JUDGE. *(handing her the bottle)* Well it's about time.

FUDGIE. *(takes huge swig, hands bottle back)* Mmm. Minty. Now what were you saying, young man?

PROSECUTOR. Please tell the court your name and your relationship to the defendant.

FUDGIE. I am known as Fudge Girl, familiarly as Fudgie, officially as Queen Fudgie the First and on rare but profitable occasions as Betty Two-Times, the Tallahassee Tease. But my name, ah, my name is a mystery. A name, a string of syllables, a conjunction of spit and breath and friction, can it evoke one's essence, can it touch one's central truth, can it even point towards one's true and hidden face? A name is a name is a name, young man, what's yours and how about a quickie?

PROSECUTOR. Let the record show the witness has identified herself as Queen Fudgie. And your relationship to the accused?

FUDGIE. The whom?

PROSECUTOR. The accused. The defendant. The fat man there in chains.

FUDGIE. Oh. Hmm. I don't…I don't believe…no, I've never met the man.

FATBOY. LIES!

FUDGIE. FAT BASTARD!

JUDGE. SILENCE! So what are you doing later?

PROSECUTOR. The witness is reminded that we have a warehouse of photographs, audiocassettes, newspaper clippings and motion pictures documenting her long and involved relationship with the accused as well as her own signed and notarized confession of her criminal awareness and involvement with the accused's activities.

FUDGIE. You make my blood boil, young man. Show a little chest.

PROSECUTOR. Can you identify the accused as the monster Fatboy?

FUDGIE. Whatever you wish, my sweet.

PROSECUTOR. And you can attest to his foul and monstrous deeds?

FUDGIE. If it would make you happy, you saucy little dish.

PROSECUTOR. Can you answer yes or no?

FUDGIE. Yes, you beauty, yes, I say yes to you, yes yes.

FATBOY. Must I sit here and watch the display of this woman's wanton ways?

FUDGIE. And yes to you, fat bastard.

FATBOY. HARLOT!

FUDGIE. MONSTER!

FATBOY. WOMAN!

FUDGIE. MAN!

JUDGE. Can anyone break a twenty? No? Proceed.

PROSECUTOR. Is this Fatboy?

FUDGIE. Yes.

PROSECUTOR. Is he a scourge, a pestilence and a plague?

FUDGIE. Yes and yes and yes.

PROSECUTOR. Is he guilty of all the crimes charged to him and many more besides?

FUDGIE. O yes, you magnificent man.

PROSECUTOR. No further questions, your honor.

JUDGE. The accused may cross-examine.

FATBOY. Your honor, I move that I get to wear your wig for awhile.

JUDGE. For what reason?

FATBOY. I believe it will make me look younger.

JUDGE. Sustained.

FATBOY. Thank you, fucker. May I wear it backwards?

JUDGE. That I cannot allow.

FATBOY. Fuck you, then. I withdraw my initial request.

JUDGE. Let the record state that the initial request has been withdrawn.

FATBOY. And that his honor is a peevish asshole.

JUDGE. And that I, though honorable, am a peevish asshole.

FATBOY. I object, your honor. Your honor is an honary term and has no bearing on your honor's actual honor.

JUDGE. Let the record state that though my honor is in doubt, my title shall remain your honor.

FATBOY. Thank you, fuckface.

JUDGE. You still want the wig?

FATBOY. I'm good, thanks.

JUDGE. Proceed.

FATBOY. So you claim to know me, woman?

FUDGIE. O shut it, you fat bastard.

FATBOY. You claim to know *me*. Fatboy the King.

FUDGIE. I knew you when you were Fatty Fatpants, the little fatty fuck.

FATBOY. Ah. Those days were golden.

FUDGIE. We laughed and ate and grew large and sullen.

FATBOY. We did not know the cares to come.

FUDGIE. We lived as though in a dream, a reverie of our own.

FATBOY. I often think back on that time and shudder for things not done.

FUDGIE. Do you have regrets, monster?

FATBOY. I could have killed you when first we met and then we wouldn't be standing here.

FUDGIE. True, but what a story we've made.

FATBOY. True, you wretch, true. Now then. Where were you on the night of the twenty-seventh?

FUDGIE. Clubfooted Christ, not this again.

FATBOY. Answer the question, woman.

FUDGIE. You know where I was. I was home with you in misery and squalor and filth.

FATBOY. And what were you doing at the time?

FUDGIE. Feeding your fat face with a lovely ham.

FATBOY. Ham, you say?

FUDGIE. Yes.

FATBOY. HAM! JESUS, HAM! SWEET SAVORY SKIN OF THE PIG! And what else was on the menu?

FUDGIE. You know what was on the menu.

FATBOY. Tell the court, whore.

FUDGIE. Pancakes, you pig.

FATBOY. HOW MANY PANCAKES?

FUDGIE. I MADE THREE AND YOU ATE TWO OF THEM!

FATBOY. YOU MADE FOUR AND KEPT HALF FOR YOURSELF! ADMIT IT AND THE COURT WILL SHOW MERCY!

FUDGIE. You fat bastard. I told you. I only made three.

FATBOY. LIAR!

FUDGIE. And I had to snatch the third from your hands or I would have gone hungry that night.

FATBOY. YOU ATE MY PANCAKE!

FUDGIE. FAT FUCKER!

FATBOY. ATE MY DELICIOUS PANCAKE!

FUDGIE. I ONLY MADE THREE. Fat bastard.

FATBOY. No further questions.

JUDGE. The witness is excused.

FUDGIE. I'd just like to thank the Academy.

JUDGE. You want to sit up here with me?

FUDGIE. In a moment, yes, but first I must taste this young man.

PROSECUTOR. Ma'am, I must ask you to go.

FUDGIE. I'll come and go as you please, sir.

PROSECUTOR. I have more witnesses to question.

FUDGIE. What will they tell you that I cannot show you and now?

PROSECUTOR. This is most irregular, madam.

FUDGIE. You ain't seen nothing yet.

FATBOY. Better go with her, boy. She's a horror but she gets what she wants.

PROSECUTOR. Your honor, I request a short recess.

JUDGE. Request denied.

PROSECUTOR. But, sir –

JUDGE. You were the one being stickly earlier. I can be stickly now.

FUDGIE. I love a good stickler. Are you stickly, my sweet?

PROSECUTOR. I've stickled a few in my days.

FUDGIE. Are you stiff and unbending and harsh?

PROSECUTOR. I believe there's a proper way.

FUDGIE. A straight and narrow…path?

PROSECUTOR. Things should be done just so.

FUDGIE. Do me like things should be done, you demon!

PROSECUTOR. You siren! You vixen! You nymph!

(**FUDGIE** *drags* **PROSECUTOR** *offstage.*)

JUDGE. Don't wear her out now! Stickly? Save some for the rest! Ah well. Does anyone know any good jokes? Does anyone have a light? Can anyone recommend a reputable chiropractor? Does anyone want to see some naked pictures of my wife? No? Proceed.

FUDGIE. *(offstage)* YES, BY THE NAPPY HEAD OF JESUS!

PROSECUTOR. *(offstage)* MY GOD, WOMAN, NOT SO FAST!

BAILIFF. Your honor, I beg permission to leave the stage.

JUDGE. For what reason?

BAILIFF. I must go and change costumes, sir.

JUDGE. And what is wrong with the costume you have on?

BAILIFF. Nothing at all, sir. It is just that I am double-cast and must soon enter as another character.

JUDGE. And is the union aware of this?

BAILIFF. They are, sir.

JUDGE. Very well. We shall miss you, good bailiff.

BAILIFF. And I, you, sir.

JUDGE. Our time together has been brief and yet I feel my very heart being rent in two as I am forced to consider your leave-taking.

BAILIFF. Speak no more of it, sir, or I shall collapse to the ground and weep.

JUDGE. We must be strong and carry forward, masking our pain with resolve.

BAILIFF. I shall never forget our time here. I shall cherish it all my days.

JUDGE. Do you love me, bailiff?

BAILIFF. With all of my soul, sir.

JUDGE. Go now and leave us to our grief and sorrow.

BAILIFF. Adieu, mon cheri. Adieu.

(**BAILIFF** *exits.*)

JUDGE. A sad day for all of us, shouty.

FATBOY. Fuck his double-cast ass. At least he gets a break. I'm out here shouting the whole time.

JUDGE. True, true. Now then. No prosecutor, no bailiff. How shall we proceed?

FATBOY. I move that I be allowed to sing a little song.

JUDGE. It is so moved.

FATBOY. (*singing to the tune of the old childhood song "Three Little Fishies".*)
HEY, I'M FATBOY AND HOW ARE YOU?
YES, I'M FATBOY AND SO FUCK YOU
I'M A BIG FAT FATBOY, A BOY THAT'S FAT
FUCKYOUFUCKYOUFUCKYOUFUCKYOU, WHAT-CHA THINK OF THAT?
FATBOY
MY NAME IS FATBOY
HELLO I'M FATBOY
FUCK YOU AND YOU AND YOU

FUDGIE. *(entering from stage left)*
> HE'S FATBOY
> THE MONSTER FATBOY
> MY GOD, IT'S FATBOY
> TAKE OFF YOUR PANTS

BOTH.
> WELL, I'M FATBOY, HAVE WE MET?
> YES, HE'S FATBOY SO DON'T FORGET
> IF I WANT IT THEN I'LL TAKE AND THERE'S NOTHING YOU CAN DO
> SO BOW DOWN, FUCKERS AND HEY, FUCK YOU
>
> FATBOY
> HEY HEY I'M FATBOY
> WE'RE TALKING FATBOY
> FUCK YOU AND YOU AND YOU AND YOU

PROSECUTOR. *(entering from stage right)*
> FATBOY
> GOOD GOD IT'S FATBOY
> THAT BIG FAT FATBOY
> HE'S REALLY FAT

FATBOY.
> TALKING 'BOUT FATBOY, THAT'S MY NAME
> GLOBAL DOMINATION, THAT'S MY GAME
> JUST A BIG FAT FATBOY, CAN'T YOU SEE?
> SO GATHER UP YOUR SHIT AND GIVE IT TO ME

ALL.
> FATBOY
> FUCK YES IT'S FATBOY
> O FUCK YEAH, FATBOY
> AND NOW WE DANCE!
>
> FATBOY
> COME ON, FATBOY
> HELL YES, FATBOY
> FUCK YOU
>
> FATBOY
> GIVE IT UP FATBOY
> WE'RE TALKING FATBOY
> HE'S FUCKING FAT!

FATBOY.
AND THAT'S MY SONG!

*(**FATBOY**, **FUDGIE** and **PROSECUTOR** bow, **FUDGIE** chases **PROSECTOR** off stage left.)*

JUDGE. ORDER! ORDER! You said nothing about dancing, sir. That sort of thing is frowned on and liable to get you fined.

FATBOY. To sing and not dance is unnatural, fucker.

JUDGE. Nature is vastly overrated. Redundant, obvious and slow. Man-made for me, boy. It's worth the added cost.

FUDGIE. *(offstage)* HOLY JUMPING JUDAS!

PROSECUTOR. *(offstage)* JUST WAIT, WOMAN! HELP!

FATBOY. What now, asshole?

JUDGE. Too soon for intermission. Let's keep going.

FUDGIE. *(offstage)* YES, BY THE CHAPPED HANDS OF MARTHA!

PROSECUTOR. *(offstage)* YOU'RE HURTING ME! BAILIFF!

JUDGE. ORDER! ORDER OFFSTAGE! CALL YOUR NEXT WITNESS, STICKLY!

PROSECUTOR. *(sticking his head out)* I call a nameless innocent.

FUDGIE. *(sticking her head out)* Finish what you've started.

*(**FUDGIE** drags **PROSECUTOR** back offstage as **INNOCENT** enters stage right.)*

PROSECUTOR. FOR CHRIST'S SAKE WOMAN!

FUDGIE. DO ME DO ME DO ME!

JUDGE. Do you swear to tell the blah blah blah etc.?

INNOCENT. I swear to tell the truth.

FATBOY. THAT'S NOT WHAT HE ASKED YOU.

JUDGE. *(shouting in horror and discovery)* I'M BLIND! No, just kidding. Proceed.

FATBOY. As my esteemed colleague and accuser has shamefully abandoned the courtroom, proving himself to be the asshole coward motherfucker piece of shit that innumerable bathroom stalls throughout the land unequivocally claim him to be, I humbly request permission to question this so-called witness on his behalf. Fucker.

JUDGE. Most irregular, sir. Most irregular indeed. I like it. Proceed.

FATBOY. Your honor, I move to strike this witness.

JUDGE. Granted.

FATBOY. *(strikes* **INNOCENT***)* Thank you, your honor, I feel much better now. So, what is that we can do for you today?

INNOCENT. You destroyed my cities and murdered hundreds of thousands of innocent civilians.

FATBOY. These cities that you speak of, fuckface, where are they now?

INNOCENT. They do not exist. They are rubble.

FATBOY. Hah! So it is your contention that I have destroyed cities that do not exist?

INNOCENT. Yes, I –

FATBOY. This witness stands against all logic. His testimony is tautologically invalid.

JUDGE. Big words, shouty. Do you know what they mean?

FATBOY. I do, fuckhead.

JUDGE. Proceed then, sir.

FATBOY. And this murdered multitude you insist on. Where are these people?

INNOCENT. Their bones lie unmarked in the fields.

FATBOY. Bring them forward. Let them speak.

INNOCENT. They have no voice. Their silence is their testimony.

FATBOY. Your argument is silence? Well, mine is speech and AT GREAT VOLUME YOU WORM.

JUDGE. Shouty shouty shouty. Anyone see the game last night?

PROSECUTOR. *(Sticking his head out, he is bare-chested and exhausted.)* Your honor, I must object.

JUDGE. For what reason, sir?

PROSECUTOR. The accused is making a mockery of this most grave and serious proceeding.

JUDGE. Is this true, sir?

FATBOY. Fuck you twice, fucker.

JUDGE. Proceed.

*(**PROSECUTOR** is pulled back offstage.)*

FATBOY. Your honor, I move that this witness's testimony be ignored, expunged, erased and incinerated, the ashes to be scattered and lost for all time.

JUDGE. For what reason?

FATBOY. Your honor, the witness is a Jew.

JUDGE. I must warn you, sir. Up to now I have allowed your unorthodox behavior and approach out of a certain morbid fascination. But to impugn an individual because of that individual's religious beliefs or convictions is beyond what I can endure. It is a man's words and actions that count in this courtroom, and the prejudice and hatred of the ignorant hold no weight here.

(huge laughter bit)

FATBOY. You almost had me there at the end, you fucker.

JUDGE. Yeah, it's a good one. Request granted. Remove the Jew.

FATBOY. But first, sir, a moment.

FUDGIE. *(offstage)* YES YOU DIRTY BOY!

PROSECUTOR. *(offstage)* MY HEART! MY HEART! ACK!

FUDGIE. *(returning abruptly, staring at something awful offstage)* Oh, dear.

FATBOY. This subhuman fuck has smeared my good name. I am Fatboy, after all AND NONE DARE QUESTION.

FUDGIE. He's just having a little lie-down. It was purely consensual, I swear.

FATBOY. Killed another, did you?

FUDGIE. Stronger sex, my ass.

FATBOY. WICKED WANTON WHORE

FUDGIE. GUILTY FAT BASTARD!

JUDGE. SILENCE! Give us a kiss.

(**FUDGIE** *leaps into* **JUDGE***'s arms, they embrace and smooch and slobber through the following exchange.*)

FATBOY. Tell me, asshole, where were you born?

INNOCENT. In a village in a country that is gone.

FATBOY. And why did you leave that village?

INNOCENT. You burned it to the ground one night. The village left before I did.

FATBOY. What is it you do for a living?

INNOCENT. I labor. I scavenge. I work.

FATBOY. Good money in that?

INNOCENT. Not by your standards, monster. But I have enough to live.

FATBOY. You presume to know my standards, fuckhead?

INNOCENT. *(holding up bag)* This is all I have. It would mean nothing to you.

FATBOY. Is that money, dickhead?

INNOCENT. All that I have, sir.

FATBOY. Does anyone not see where this is going? Permission to approach the witness.

JUDGE. Are you still here? Proceed.

FATBOY. Permission to place my hands around the witness's neck.

JUDGE. Christ, man, get it over with.

FATBOY. *(strangling* **INNOCENT***)* WE WANT TO THANK YOU FOR COMING HERE TODAY. YOU HAVE SHOWN GREAT COURAGE AND CONVICTION. IS THERE ANYTHING YOU'D LIKE TO ADD?

(Snaps **INNOCENT***'s neck,* **INNOCENT** *collapses, dead.)*

Anything? Any more...accusations? Unfounded rumors or lies or baseless allegations? No? Well, then. I'll take that. *(takes bag)* Your honor, I wish to make a small donation to the upkeep of this worthy institution.

JUDGE. Are you attempting to bribe me, sir?

FATBOY. Just a gift, asshole. And by accepting the gift, you agree to absolve me of all charges.

JUDGE. That sounds suspiciously like a bribe, sir. Therefore, I direct you to follow me into my chambers and make sure that all of the money is in order, smaller denominations followed by larger denominations, all face forward and I should warn you that I can't make change.

FATBOY. Justice is immutable, sir. No change is required.

(**JUDGE** *and* **FATBOY** *exit.*)

FUDGIE. *(to audience)* Oh, I know how this must look. Shouting and horror and murder and me jumping anything that moves. But you must look at the larger picture. Look at the whole board. There's a justice at work here. Not some primitive eye for an eye, or some great moral counting-house where each small action and gesture and word is weighed on some golden scale, something simpler and more lovely than that. We must trust the ways of the Fat Man. There's a joy to his random rage. There is something deeper than law there, something more truthful than fact. And he's a great deal of fun, you must admit.

FATBOY. *(entering)* MOTHERFUCK!

FUDGIE. They took off your chains, fat bastard.

FATBOY. The outcome was never in doubt.

FUDGIE. It must feel good to breathe free.

FATBOY. If you like that sort of thing.

FUDGIE. Where did that lovely judge go?

FATBOY. Killed him. Only seemed right.

FUDGIE. So you still have the bribe money?

FATBOY. Ate it. Speaking of which –

FUDGIE. I ONLY MADE THREE.

FATBOY. You wretched, lying whore.

FUDGIE. What will they do without a judge?

FATBOY. He was merely ornamental. Judges are a thing of the past.

FUDGIE. What principle will guide us, pray tell?

FATBOY. In the end, you whore, it is strength. Some call it freedom and I say fine, I say fuck you, call it freedom, call it force, call it fuck-a-doodle-cockfuck, but its true name is Fatboy and *(singing)* THAT'S MY NAME, TOO.

FUDGIE. How will you rule, great and illustrious bastard?

FATBOY. Today, you frightful succubus, I enjoy a position of great military strength and incredible economic and political influence. In keeping with my heritage and principles, I do not use my strength to press for unilateral advantage. I use it to take what I want and destroy what I don't and terrorize the sheep and fools and fuckheads that stand against me. The war against assholes and fuckheads is a global enterprise of uncertain duration. Therefore, ask not what Fatboy can do for you, but what Fatboy wants for lunch, you fuckers. We have nothing to fear but fuckheads themselves. We shall fight them on the beaches, we shall fight them on the fields, we shall rip their fucking heads off and piss right down their throats. I will act against such emerging fuckheads before they are fully formed. YES? GET IT? You see, my friends, it's morning in America, so somebody better make me some fucking pancakes. L'etat c'est moi. Say whaaaaa? C'est moi. I am not a crook. I believe in a place called hope. Ich bin ein Berliner. Yes we can. In the new world I have created, the only path to safety is the path of action. LIGHTS. CAMERAS. AAAAAAAAAAND ACTION!

FUDGIE. You mean pre-emptive attack of merely perceived enemies, fat bastard?

FATBOY. I MEAN CONSTANT AND INCREASING BULLYING, INTIMIDATION AND LOW-LEVEL SKIRMISH UNTIL ALL SHALL BOW. You're either with me or against me.

FUDGIE. You fat, fat fucker. Who would stand with you?

FATBOY. Slaves and fools and those who perceive an advantage.

FUDGIE. *(with enormous derision) Them.*

FATBOY. They shall snap at my heels like toothless dogs and I shall lead them to their graves.

FUDGIE. Are they many?

FATBOY. They are legion. Their numbers grow by the day. Now go and find me some food.

FUDGIE. I am not some cross-eyed domestic. I am Queen Fudgie the First.

FATBOY. Someday I'll have a second.

FUDGIE. Over my dead body.

FATBOY. Precisely, you horrible cow.

FUDGIE. Don't you try.

FATBOY. Come here, my poisonous sweet.

FUDGIE. I'll kick your ass, man.

FATBOY. WHORE!

FUDGIE. FAT BASTARD!

(They rush at each other, screaming and grapple as the curtain falls.)

SECOND ENTR'ACTE

*(**FATBOY** and **FUDGIE** step out as before.)*

FATBOY. We have received numerous telegrams, faxes, emails and hand-written missives during the course of the performance congratulating us on our success and over and over our adoring public has asked, "How on earth did the two of you meet and could you possibly perform a prequel?"

FUDGIE. And in response to Mr. Rodriguez's lurid query I would just like to say yes, you naughty man, once in Acapulco.

FATBOY. A prequel would, sadly, be impossible, for the amount of make-up required to give my wife the impression of youth would render her face immobile and quite possibly the weight of it would snap her neck. I am, of course, all for the possibility of a snapped neck, however, my esteemed spouse, the objectionable cow, has demurred. It seems we have another act to perform and the management has not supplied us with an understudy.

FUDGIE. Or a dressing room.

FATBOY. Or any reason to believe we shall be paid.

FUDGIE. Thieves.

FATBOY. Unscrupulous cocksucking pricks

FUDGIE. Theater owners and operators.

FATBOY. We have, therefore, hit upon the ingenious solution of presenting our meeting, courtship and early years in the form of a traditional puppet show.

(Puppet stage is brought out, they stand behind it and draw curtain, revealing two hand puppets bearing a rough resemblance to themselves.)

FUDGIE. Here I am, a blameless virgin, the very model of modesty and virtue, standing alone on a bright sunny day in this nondescript town, ah me. I wonder what the day will bring.

FATBOY. Why is my puppet so fat?

FUDGIE. I believe they're going for realism.

FATBOY. Seems a little late in the day for that.

FUDGIE. Shut up and do the play.

FATBOY. *(entering)* Dope-dee-dope-dee-dope-dee-doo. Well, hello young lady!

FUDGIE. Hello, you pudgy little boy!

FATBOY. I'm not pudgy.

FUDGIE. Hello, you husky little fatty fatty!

FATBOY. Don't call me fat!

FUDGIE. Hello! OK? Hello. Now do your line.

FATBOY. This doesn't look anything like me. (**FATBOY** *examines his puppet closely, sniffs it and begins to eat it.*)

FUDGIE. Don't eat the puppet!

FATBOY. I HAVE TO KEEP UP MY STRENGTH! *(He takes an enormous bite out of the puppet stage.)*

FUDGIE. FAT FUCKER!

FATBOY. WHORE!

(They begin to grapple as large hooks, as before, drag them off the stage. The puppet stage stands alone. After a moment, the actor playing the **TENANT** *and the* **PROSECUTOR** *steps out, wordlessly apologizes to the audience and removes the puppet stage.)*

FATBOY, FATBOY UBER ALLES

(**FATBOY**, *wearing crown, stands in front of throne, Ministers and* **SLAVE** *bow before him.*)

ALL. All hail Fatboy!

FATBOY. Arise, dear fuckheads and kiss my fucking ass.

(They do so through the following speech.)

Methinks, ay me, I shall now speak like thus.
'Tis fitting that one so grand and large as I
Should sound as if I had a fucking clue
As how to rule with grace and style and class.
For though the hungry beast may roar within
Without the words should sound as temple bells.
What say thee, ye suckers of many a cock?

MINISTER OF FINANCE. In sooth, sir –

FATBOY. Nay, nay, speak as before
And in that way we shall know who is king.

SLAVE. You...sound great, your majesty.

FATBOY. Thou sayst so in the vernacular?

SLAVE. Yes, your majesty. I'm just saying.

FATBOY. 'Tis pleasing on the ear to speak like this.
The honeyed words do roll out on the tongue
And seem to kiss the lips of him who speaks
And even "motherfuck" and "fucking shit"
Are gentled by the rhythm of the verse.
But tell me and be honest, dear fuckheads
Does it in any way make me seem gay?

SLAVE. Umm. No, sir.

FATBOY. A bit of sport with those of like same sex
Is not a thing to shudder at, of course.
Indeed, perhaps you all shall suck my cock
Before our revelries have here drawn nigh.

MINISTER OF JUSTICE. This is starting to creep me out a bit.

SLAVE. Yeah, me too.

FATBOY. Forsooth! Forsooth thou fuckers of thine own
    Mother's wombs. 'Tis now the third and final
    Act and we shall wax poetic ere we die.

MINISTER OF FINANCE. Die, your highness?

FATBOY. Did I say "die"? The word itself betrays.
    But words once spoken can in time come true.
    And though the mighty earth itself may crack
    And mountains vanish into hungry seas
    The end of one man's life, be thou that man,
    Is greater than the ending of the world.
    You two, leave the stage. You stay here with me.
    Off, you motherfuckers, exeunt both.

MINISTER OF JUSTICE. We'll just be backstage.

MINISTER OF FINANCE. Call us if you need anything.

FATBOY. Leave me with my slave.

    (The ministers exit. An uncomfortable moment.)

SLAVE. How's it going, sir?

FATBOY. My life is like a pageant or a play
    And when the curtain falls for the last time
    What waits beyond yon great and groaning-
    Ah fuck this, bring me some pancakes, fucker.

SLAVE. About the pancakes, sir.

FATBOY. Don't start that cholesterol bullshit with me.

SLAVE. No, no, it's not the cholesterol, sir, it's just…

FATBOY. What, fucker? I'm hungry and you're standing
    here talking.

SLAVE. You have eaten every pancake in the world, sir.

FATBOY. I have eaten every pancake in the world?

SLAVE. And I congratulate you on your remarkable success.

FATBOY. That doesn't even make any sense. Make fresh pancakes.

SLAVE. Sir, you have eaten every grain of wheat and
    neglected to water the fields. You have fried every fowl
    and so there are no eggs. You've barbecued every steer

and roasted every goat. Milk has become a memory. How about some dry granola?

FATBOY. Hurts my teeth.

SLAVE. A little grapefruit, maybe?

FATBOY. Too tart, fucker, too tart. Bring me bacon and sausage and ham.

SLAVE. Ah, there's a problem there, your enormous majesty.

FATBOY. Problems aren't my problem, pal.

SLAVE. This one, sadly, affects you.

FATBOY. What is the point of being king if I still have to stand around with assholes like you and discuss my diet?

SLAVE. It's a riddle, sir, a great one.

FATBOY. Tell me the problem, fuckface.

SLAVE. You've eaten all the pigs. Swine are off the menu. The Muslims thank you, sir.

FATBOY. No pigs?

SLAVE. No more.

FATBOY. No sweet little piggies?

SLAVE. Gone, sir. History.

FATBOY. I WANT PIG!

SLAVE. I know, sir, I'm sorry.

FATBOY. GIVE ME PIGGY PIGGY!

SLAVE. Piggy's gone away, sir, I'm sorry. Have some grapes.

FATBOY. No cows no pigs no chickens. No wheat?

SLAVE. No wheat.

FATBOY. No wheat. Jesus Christ, I'll starve. How is this possible? SOMEBODY FUCKED UP, FUCKER! Someone has betrayed me. An enemy within. *(He begins to absent-mindedly eat his crown.)* They play the willing servants, but secretly they scheme. I'M EATING MY CROWN! HAS IT COME TO THIS? *(He continues snacking on crown.)* They tremble in my presence and mock me when I'm gone. Cocksuckers. Fuckheaded cocksucking mother-fucking fucks. They don't love me. Not really. Not one of them down deep. Do you love me, fuckhead?

SLAVE. No sir.

FATBOY. ANSWER THE QUESTION.

SLAVE. I said no, sir, no, I don't.

FATBOY. Dodges and double-talk. Can no one speak straight to me now? Is my wife about?

SLAVE. Just off-stage, sir.

FATBOY. Send her rotten, wretched carcass in.

SLAVE. At once, sir, at once.

FATBOY. WAIT. Kiss my ass.

SLAVE. Sir?

FATBOY. KISS MY ASS NOW YOU WORTHLESS SACK OF SHIT.

*(He kneels and kisses **FATBOY**'s ass.)*

FATBOY. Ass-kisser.

SLAVE. Yes, sir.

FATBOY. Exit now.

SLAVE. O yes, sir.

(He exits.)

FATBOY. At the height of my powers and I can't get a pancake. The peak of my form and no pork to eat. What a load of fucking crap. I AM FATBOY AND I AM HUNGRY. Was I to water the fields? Count every chicken, cow and sheep? Not devour all and everything simply because it was there and I wanted it? What kind of motherfucking horseshit cocksucking bullshit is that? But soft, I am o'erheard.

*(**FUDGIE** enters, wearing a crown.)*

FUDGIE. My king.

FATBOY. My queen.

FUDGIE. Fat bastard.

FATBOY. Whore.

FUDGIE. Have you seen the larger than life statue they have made of you in town?

FATBOY. I have. It does not please me.

FUDGIE. Why not, you horrible man?

FATBOY. It makes me look fat.

FUDGIE. There should be more statues of me.

FATBOY. To frighten little children and guard the city gates?

FUDGIE. So those who wish can worship with convenience and not have to trek across town.

FATBOY. Is it worship you wish, wretched woman?

FUDGIE. What else is there finally, fat man?

FATBOY. Dignity. Honor. Love.

(**FUDGIE** *explodes into huge laughter,* **FATBOY** *does not.*)

FUDGIE. Ah, you fat fucker. You could always make me laugh.

FATBOY. It seems I've laid waste to the world.

FUDGIE. Yes, I know, fat bastard.

FATBOY. An ocean of blood, a mountain range of bones, and for what, you aged slattern?

FUDGIE. It seemed to pass the time.

FATBOY. True, you whore, but now that it's passed I am empty as though never filled, my hunger a gentle lapping where once it roared and crashed.

FUDGIE. Well, you're old, you fat bastard. This happens when you age.

FATBOY. I don't wish to be old.

FUDGIE. You age and then you age and then you age and then you die.

FATBOY. I don't wish to die.

FUDGIE. No way out of here alive, fat fucker.

FATBOY. This is an outrage. This will not stand.

FUDGIE. Nor will you when you die, monster. You'll be splayed out on the floor and we'll all shout Fatboy is Dead, Long Live Fatboy! Wait a minute, that doesn't make any sense, does it? Fatboy is Dead, Long Live Fudgie. Yes. Better. We'll dance around your rotting corpse and call you awful names and the reign of Queen Fudgie the Good will begin.

FATBOY. The Good? But you're loathsome and vile and... *bad.*

FUDGIE. I can be good if I want.

FATBOY. Never. Not possible. No.

FUDGIE. I CAN BE GOOD.

FATBOY. YOUR EVERY THOUGHT IS SIN.

FUDGIE. OLD DYING BASTARD!

FATBOY. SINFUL WRETCHED WHORE!

FUDGIE. KILL HIM NOW! *(Silence. An uncomfortable pause as* **FUDGIE** *looks around the stage.)* I said, KILL HIM NOW! *(another pause)*

FATBOY. Who are you talking to?

FUDGIE. Hmm? Oh. I was just calling my…assistant. Kelly. Kelly…Mnyow.

FATBOY. Mnyow?

FUDGIE. Yes. She's Vietnamese. Cantonese. Szechuann.

FATBOY. I don't think I've met her.

FUDGIE. No, she's new.

FATBOY. Ah.

FUDGIE. Must not be within earshot.

FATBOY. No.

FUDGIE. Ah well. I'm going to go get laid.

FATBOY. Wait. Don't leave me, you horrible woman.

FUDGIE. Why I left you years ago, fucker. Are you just noticing now?

 *(***FUDGIE** *exits.)*

FATBOY. Whore. Once I grew warm when we battled. Now it's like a wind-up toy. FUCKHEAD!

 *(***SLAVE** *scurries on, prostrates himself.)*

SLAVE. Yes o monstrous Fatboy.

FATBOY. Stand here while I soliloquize.

SLAVE. With joy and reverence, sir.

FATBOY. I feel the end of something. I fear the end of all. My will, once certain, now wavers. My force flickers and dims. There is no joy in destruction. There is no point in creation. There is only endurance. And strength.

But this will eventually wear. And then…then, what?
An old and feeble Fatboy? Laughed at, pushed aside,
jeered and then forgotten? O no. It must not happen.
I must break the cycle of time. I must stop the pen-
dulum from swinging and freeze it here, triumphant.
The only way to protect my legacy is to kill everyone
I've ever known. Yes. All my contemporaries vanished.
But then, still, still, then, future generations may look
at what I've done and judge me harshly. Fuckers. Cocksucking unborn judgemental fuckers. They must not
be allowed. They must die before birth, before con-
ception, unmade. Ah. All must die. Only then may I
breathe free. That's it then. ASSHOLE!

SLAVE. Yes sir.

FATBOY. Kill everything that lives and then kill yourself
when you're done.

SLAVE. Yes, your majesty. *(He goes to exit and then stops.)* Your
majesty?

FATBOY. Fucker?

SLAVE. By everything, you mean everyone?

FATBOY. Thing, slave, thing. Kill every thing. If life can
grow, it may grow sentient. Future races of complex
life forms must not be allowed to thrive and discover
my deeds. Some bacterial infection must be prevented
from in time mutating and evolving in to something
that can think and speak and slander my good name.

SLAVE. Got it. Kill all things.

FATBOY. And then kill yourself.

SLAVE. Of course, sir. Thank you.

FATBOY. Now go. WAIT. Kiss my ass.

SLAVE. Again, sir?

FATBOY. Again and again, fucker, until it's second nature.

(SLAVE kisses FATBOY's ass.)

FATBOY. Ass-kisser.

SLAVE. Well, yes sir.

FATBOY. Kisser of my ass.

SLAVE. Will that be all, sir?

FATBOY. Yes. No. Kiss my ass.

SLAVE. But, sir –

FATBOY. Kiss my ass, fucker.

SLAVE. Jesus, sir, I just –

FATBOY. KISS KISS KISS MY ASS ASS ASS. You fucking ass-kissing fucking fuck.

(**SLAVE** *kisses* **FATBOY***'s ass again.*)

FATBOY. You kissed my ass, fucker.

SLAVE. Yes, sir, I did.

FATBOY. That would make you an ass-kisser.

SLAVE. Yes, sir, it would.

FATBOY. All right. Just making sure.

SLAVE. I have to go now and kill everything.

FATBOY. Of course, you ass-kissing fuck. And then kill yourself.

SLAVE. Of course, sir. *(He hesitates, afraid he will be asked to kiss the ass of* **FATBOY** *again.)* I'm going now.

FATBOY. Well, go then, fucker.

SLAVE. *(exiting, sotto voce)* What a fucking prick.

FATBOY. Something seems to be troubling my slave. A note of discontent. Strange. Ah well. Perhaps I should have asked him to kiss my ass again, he seems to enjoy that. Ah well. So hard to tell what people are thinking. You have to ask them, of course, but that's not the end of it, no. Then you have to *listen.* As they drone on and on about *themselves.* "I think blah blah blah, I feel blah blah blah." JESUS FUCKING CHRIST. One could spend one's life listening to other's words.

(**FUDGIE** *enters, theatrically shielding her eyes with her forearm.*)

FUDGIE. Is it over, my beautiful boy?

FATBOY. What?

FUDGIE. Oh. It's you. I thought…hmm. Everything all right?

FATBOY. Fine, yes. Why?

FUDGIE. Were there some men in here, with knives and such…stabbing and killing you?

FATBOY. No. Why?

FUDGIE. No reason. No…assassination?

FATBOY. Not that I'm aware of, no.

FUDGIE. Huh. Funny. All right. See you later, fucker.

FATBOY. Bye. (**FUDGIE** *exits.*) That was weird. Anyway. Well, soon it will be over. Everything dead, killed. Me, alone, triumphant. Man, that's going to be nice. Breathe a little easier, that's for goddamn sure. I wonder, flood or fire? Doesn't really matter, I suppose. Fire more dramatic. Flood more Biblical, though. All the same in the end. What could be keeping that slave?

(**SLAVE** *enters with* **MINISTER OF FINANCE** *and* **MINISTER OF JUSTICE,** *all hiding something behind their back.*)

SLAVE. Sir, I have discussed your plan of complete global destruction with the Minister of Justice and the Minister of Finance.

FATBOY. It is not a plan, fuckhead. It is an order. It requires no discussion.

MINISTER OF FINANCE. Of course, your majesty, but just the same –

MINISTER OF JUSTICE. I believe we have hit upon an alternate course of action.

FATBOY. Yes?

MINISTER OF FINANCE. Yes.

SLAVE. It goes something like this. SIC SEMPER TYRANNIS!

MINISTER OF JUSTICE. DEATH TO THE FAT MAN!

MINISTER OF FINANCE. STAB HIM IN HIS FUCKING HEAD!

FATBOY. Now this is more like it.

(*They rush* **FATBOY,** *knives drawn and fight, horribly.* **MINISTER OF FINANCE** *is killed,* **FATBOY** *grapples with* **SLAVE** *and* **MINISTER OF JUSTICE,** **SLAVE** *chokes* **FATBOY,** *who gasps,*)

FATBOY. Et tu, fuckhead?

> (*And* **FATBOY** *collapses.* **SLAVE** *and* **MINISTER OF JUS-**
> **TICE** *gather downstage.*)

MINISTER OF JUSTICE. The fat fucker is dead.

SLAVE. We can all breathe free.

MINISTER OF JUSTICE. The yoke of oppression is lifted.

SLAVE. The boot removed from our throats.

MINISTER OF JUSTICE. I think I broke a nail.

SLAVE. We must go and tell the people.

MINISTER OF JUSTICE. A new day dawns.

> (**FATBOY** *rises, unseen.*)

SLAVE. We have struck a blow today, my friend.

MINISTER OF JUSTICE. Yeah, broke it. Fuck.

SLAVE. A mighty blow for justice. We have –

FATBOY. INCOMPETENT WOULD-BE ASSASSINS!

MINISTER OF JUSTICE. SUPPOSED TO BE DEAD MOTHER-
FUCKER!

> (*They fight,* **MINISTER OF JUSTICE** *is killed,* **FATBOY**
> *collapses,* **SLAVE** *crosses downstage.*)

SLAVE. The fat fucker is strong.

> (**FUDGIE** *enters as before.*)

FUDGIE. Is it over, my beautiful boy?

SLAVE. No. It has begun.

FUDGIE. Look at the lovely bodies strewn. Very Eliza-
bethian.

SLAVE. Their blood anoints a new age.

FUDGIE. And mine beats strong for you.

SLAVE. Come to me, my vixen.

FUDGIE. Ah, you murdering slave.

> (**FATBOY** *rises, unseen.*)

SLAVE. I shall rule with justice.

FUDGIE. No, boy. I shall rule alone.

FATBOY. NON-ASSASSINATING FUCK!

SLAVE. NON-DYING HORROR MOVIE MONSTER!

(They fight, horribly, both collapse.)

SLAVE. I tried. Tell them I tried.

FUDGIE. I shall tell them you failed. If I mention you at all.

SLAVE. Tell them –

FUDGIE. Hush now, failure.

*(She snaps **SLAVE**'s neck.)*

FUDGIE. And you, fucker? Any last words?

FATBOY. MOTHERFUCK!

FUDGIE. Yes, to balance the beginning. You always had a way with words.

FATBOY. The light grows dim.

FUDGIE. It's dark where you're going.

FATBOY. Stay with me while I die.

FUDGIE. Is it going to be a while?

FATBOY. Did I leave the world a better place?

FUDGIE. No, you bastard, you didn't.

FATBOY. Did I do some good in this world?

FUDGIE. No, you horror, none.

FATBOY. Am I a good man or a bad man?

FUDGIE. A very bad man, monster. The worst I've ever known.

FATBOY. And how will I be judged?

FUDGIE. Guilty on all counts.

FATBOY. Motherfuck. *(collapses)*

FUDGIE. Fatboy is dead. Long live Fatboy. No, wait a minute, that doesn't make any sense, does it? Fatboy is dead. Long live Fudgie. Yes. Better. My reign shall be better. Or not. Different, I suppose. Or not. We'll see. The important thing is that I'm still standing. And all that the fat fucker fought for is mine now, outright. Hah. You forgot what I told you in the beginning, didn't you? Before all the shouting and blood. I am the brains of this outfit. I played him like a pawn. We

women watch, you fuckers. We see the game unfold.
All you men with your wee wilted willies and your
nervous little sphincters shut tight. Strutting about
all grim and serious making laws, wars, headlines. We
wave you off to battle and wait to see who returns. And
that one then becomes our toy, our tool to advance a
little further.

(**FATBOY** *rises up behind her, knife in hand, and begins
to creep towards her.*)

The fat boy was my fool. A burden I've carried and
now lay down. I shall erase him from the history books,
none shall know he lived. I spit on his-

(**FATBOY** *grabs her from behind, spins her around and
stabs her repeatedly. She screams horribly and then they
both stop and turn to look out at us. She suddenly grabs
him around the neck, choking him. They struggle and
again stop, sigh deeply and look out at us again.*)

FATBOY. *(mock growling)* "Rahr rahr rahr"

FUDGIE. *(soft, mocking)* "Fat fucker! No!"

FATBOY. *(looking out)* "Whore!"

FUDGIE. *(looking out)* "Monster."

BOTH. *(mocking the act of fighting)* "Rahr rahr rahr!"

(*They begin to remove their costumes with the help of the
cast.*)

FATBOY. That's enough of that, I suppose.

FUDGIE. Becomes a bit predictable, pig.

FATBOY. One note, you wanton wretch?

FUDGIE. And a flat one at that.

FATBOY. Yes, well, just giving the folks a laugh. I mean,
poor fuckers, they work hard. Slaving away all day.

FUDGIE. Who slaves, monster?

FATBOY. The people. Folks. *(gesturing to audience)* Them.

FUDGIE. *(dismissively)* Them.

FATBOY. Give them a laugh, I say. Sing a little song. Shout
and jump about. Kill a few innocent people.

FUDGIE. I was innocent once.

FATBOY. You were born with a silver cock-ring in your mouth.

FUDGIE. "Fat bastard."

FATBOY. "Whore."

BOTH: "Rahr rahr rahr."

(They are now out of costume, make-up wiped off, cast standing around them.)

FATBOY. Yes, well. An epilogue, then. A closing, rousing speech. Hmm. I got nothing.

FUDGIE. Do the bit from the second act.

FATBOY. I don't believe in repeating myself.

(The entire cast does the huge laughter bit softly, mockingly.)

FUDGIE. "Ah you fat fucker, you could always blah blah blah"

FATBOY. Here's something. Yes. None of this is real. Monsters don't exist. Nothing to worry about. Life is a beautiful thing. And everyone feels that way. Everyone is happy. And everyone is good. If you see people that don't seem happy, well, something's wrong with them. They should see a doctor, get some happy pills. If you're not feeling happy, same thing for you. It's just a chemical imbalance, nine times out of ten. They can fix that now. Everyone can be happy. And if you see some suffering out there, remember, it's not your fault. You're good, you're fine, you're done. Fuck them if they're not happy, not your fucking fault. Big things, like poverty or war or whatnot, well, it's like the weather. You don't try to keep the rain from falling, right? You just go inside 'til it's over. What are you going to do, change the world? Of course not. I'll take care of that. I mean, they will. The folks in charge. They're all good people, the bosses, they're the best ones, actually. That's why they're in charge. They know better than you. Just go the fuck inside. I'll take care of everything.

You fucking sheep. You slaves. GO HOME. AND WAIT FOR MY ORDERS. NASTY WEATHER OUT. And if you don't hear from me for awhile, well I've got things to do, haven't I? I'm a busy, busy man. With all the affairs of state. It's not easy being in charge, you know, and your constant questioning and voting and protesting and all that fucking SHIT is wasting my fucking time. Just stop it. Just give up already. I've won. I AM FATBOY AND I AM EVERYWHERE. Open up a paper. Turn on the T.V. Walk around your towns, you fuckers. See anything familiar? Look at your neighbor closely the next time you say hello. Look beneath the surface. That's where I live. You think he's your friend? Think he's got your back? Wait until the tanks roll in and the buildings start to fall and somebody has to die. Is your friend going to step up? Your friend is Fatboy and he says "no." Just look in the mirror, fucker. Early in the morning or very late at night. When it's quiet and you're alone. I'll be waving back at you. I'll say BOO. I am Fatboy and I am you. I am Fatboy. I do not die. I am Fatboy, you cocksucking fuckheads. I AM FATBOY. And I'm outta here. I am *hiiiiiiiiiiiiisssss-tory!*

(lights down suddenly)

End of Play

PROPERTY LIST

ACT I
Newspaper
Envelope with edible check
Clipboard
Pen
Collapsible Top Hat
Large sack of bloody money
Small sack of coins

Entr' Acte I
John Clancy note
Huge hooks

ACT II
Gavel
Charges list
Bottle and 2 glasses
Bag of coins

Entr' Acte II
Rolling puppet stage
2 hand puppets, resembling Fatboy & Fudgie
2 small hooks for the puppets
2 huge hooks

ACT III
Edible crown
3 knives

General prop: Blood and tissues to wipe off make-up at the end of
ACT III.

From the Reviews of
FATBOY...

"Clancy's 2004 Edinburgh Fringe hit adaptation of Alfred Jarry's *Ubu Roi* comes just in time for the Wall Street meltdown and one of the most surreal election campaigns in American history."
- Steven Leigh Morris, *LA Weekly*

"A gleefully rule-breaking Punch-and-Judy show...Funny as hell."
- *Time Out Chicago*

OTHER TITLES AVAILABLE FROM SAMUEL FRENCH

DEAD CITY
Sheila Callaghan

Full Length / Comic Drama / 3m, 4f / Unit Set

It's June 16, 2004. Samantha Blossom, a chipper woman in her 40s, wakes up one June morning in her Upper East Side apartment to find her life being narrated over the airwaves of public radio. She discovers in the mail an envelope addressed to her husband from his lover, which spins her raw and untethered into an odyssey through the city…a day full of chance encounters, coincidences, a quick love affair, and a fixation on the mysterious Jewel Jupiter. Jewel, the young but damaged poet genius, eventually takes a shine to Samantha and brings her on a midnight tour of the meat-packing district which changes Samantha's life forever—or doesn't. This 90 minute comic drama is a modernized, gender-reversed, relocated, hyper-theatrical riff on the novel *Ulysses*, occurring exactly 100 years to the day after Joyce's jaunt through Dublin.

"Wonderful…Sheila Callaghan's pleasingly witty and theatrical new drama that is a love letter to New York masquerading as hate mail…[Callaghan] writes with a world-weary tone and has a poet's gift for economical description.
The entire dead city comes alive…"
- *The New York Times*

"*Dead City,* Sheila Callaghan's riff on James Joyce's *Ulysses* is stylish, lyrical, fascinating, occasionally irritating, and eminently worthwhile…the kind of work that is thoroughly invigorating."
- *Back Stage*

SAMUELFRENCH.COM

DISCARDED

Breinigsville, PA USA
03 January 2009
230061BV00005B/2/P